Dav: to the Arctic Winter Games

WRITTEN BY
Ryan Lahti

ILLUSTRATED BY
Shannon Potratz

Table of Contents

CHAPTER 1
Naujaat...5

CHAPTER 2
Michael..10

CHAPTER 3
Alvin..17

CHAPTER 4
Tryouts..24

CHAPTER 5
Practice...34

CHAPTER 6
Heading to Alberta.............................40

CHAPTER 7
Cheeseburgers...................................46

CHAPTER 8
Round Robin......................................55

CHAPTER 9
The Gold-Medal Game......................60

CHAPTER 10
Bringing Home the Gold....................70

Inuktitut Glossary...............................73

CHAPTER 1
Naujaat

I pulled my pillow over my head and groaned. "*Anaana*, could I have a few more minutes of sleep?" Getting up for school in the morning was always hard.

"Davidee Kopak!" Anaana said. "You were up way too late playing video games. It's affecting your school! It's time to get up, or you'll be late."

I got out of bed. I barely had enough time to wolf down some breakfast and get ready before Anaana hustled me out the door.

I walked toward Tuugaalik High School. It was October, and I could feel the cold Naujaat air on my face. I wished I'd brought my Jerry Cans sweatshirt to keep warm.

I always managed to catch up with my friend Jason on the walk to school. He was pretty slow.

"Wanna play hockey after school?" Jason excitedly asked me. Most days, Jason and I played hockey with our friends after school. Lately, I hadn't joined them. We played under the Arctic Circle Monument. The monument was a giant arch that marked where the Arctic Circle was. It also happened to be shaped like a hockey net. The kids in Naujaat made use of that. I played goalie. My friends would shoot pucks, tennis balls, rocks, and even pop cans at me. I'd try to shut them out like Carey Price with my Montreal Canadiens baseball cap.

"I don't really feel like it," I mumbled.

"Again? What's with you, man?" Jason asked.

I used to get very excited to play hockey. Recently, I just hadn't felt interested. "I just wanna stay home and play video games tonight," I told him.

Life in Naujaat revolves around hockey, and I used to love it. The arena had naturally frozen ice for most of the year. The stands were always filled with cheering fans. In the summer months,

people played floor hockey at the high school. I was a strong goalie. Most people in Naujaat had seen me play.

But nobody knew about me outside my community. Hockey players from Naujaat almost never played teams from other communities. Lately, I'd been having trouble finding a reason to keep playing. I knew that one day, I'd be old enough to try out for the territorial hockey tournament, the Polar Bear Plate. That used to keep me going, the dream of playing in front of the huge crowds in Rankin Inlet at the junior men's tournament. It was always amazing hockey. I'd even gone to Rankin Inlet to watch it in person before. Other years, I followed the score updates on Facebook with my anaana.

"I just don't know about hockey anymore," I said. "I mean, what's the point? We practise every day, but the Polar Bear Plate is a million years away for us. I just wish we could play against other teams, you know? See how good we really are."

"If you stop playing, you'll get even slower than you already are," Jason joked. I snorted. We both knew I was fast. Jason continued, "You need to stay in shape. You never know when the next hockey opportunity will come up. Maybe one day, the Montreal Canadiens will need a new goalie."

"You're right," I agreed. "One day, I'm going to play hockey in the NHL. I'll be the first player from Naujaat to play in the NHL *and* win the Stanley Cup!" I was beginning to feel happier at the thought of my hockey dream.

"You won't be playing hockey anywhere if you don't practise," Jason reminded me. "So come on. Are you going to join us after school?"

"We'll see," I said. But secretly, I was already thinking about a nap and some video games.

CHAPTER 2
Michael

When we got to school, the hallways were empty except for a few students rushing to class. Jason and I were in different classes. Jason walked up the stairs to his science class. I made my way down to the noisy wood shop.

"Mr. Kopak, you made it out of bed today!" my wood shop teacher, Michael, exclaimed. He always called students by their last names when they were late. Michael had a kind smile. "You know, if you spent more time in the shop and less time sleeping, you'd have built a whole cabin by now," he teased.

"Sorry, Michael. I slept in again...but I'm here now," I said. I really looked up to Michael. Not only was he my favourite teacher, but he lived just a few houses down from me. He'd known me since I was a baby. He'd always wave to Jason and me from his 1989 Bravo when we were playing hockey.

My class was making shelves out of old wooden pallets. I had fallen behind. I worked hard on my shelf for the rest of the class, hoping for Michael's approval.

"Would you look at that?" Michael said as he held up my shelf. The glue was still a little wet, and one edge needed more sanding, but it was almost finished. "I'm stunned you were able to pull this off today."

The bell rang, and my classmates cleared out of the shop. I stayed back to continue chatting with Michael. "I've been exhausted lately," I groaned.

"Exhausted, huh? Your anaana tells me that you've been staying up late playing video games on school nights. Is that why you're always so tired? Is that why you had to race to build this shelf today?" Michael asked.

"She...she told you that?" I asked, feeling a rush of embarrassment. I knew my anaana chatted with Michael, but I couldn't believe she'd told my teacher I was always playing video games. "Well, I don't care," I said. "I like playing video games."

"Are you still playing hockey?" asked Michael.

I shrugged and tipped my chin up. "What's

the point in playing hockey anymore? There's no challenge!"

Without saying anything, Michael walked over to his cluttered desk and began sorting through papers until he found what he was looking for. He walked back over to my workbench and placed down a flyer that read:

ARCTIC WINTER GAMES
HOCKEY TRYOUTS—RANKIN INLET
NOVEMBER 20TH

The flyer had a picture of a hockey player wearing a Nunavut jersey with vibrant yellow, red, and blue colours. There was information about the upcoming tryouts in Rankin Inlet. They were just a few weeks away.

"Arctic Winter Games hockey tryouts? Are you kidding me?" I laughed. "I heard they only choose players from Baffin Island." Just as I started to crumple up the flyer, Michael stopped me.

"What are you doing? Why are you ruining my flyer?" he asked.

"Because I'm probably not good enough to make the team!" I griped as I stormed out of the wood shop.

Michael walked over to the wood shop's front door and called to me down the hallway: "You know, I played in the 2000 Arctic Winter Games."

I stopped stamping my feet and slowly turned around.

Michael continued, "We weren't the best, but it felt so good to wear the Team Nunavut jersey and represent not just the territory but Naujaat as well." Michael looked at me. "We ended up losing in the gold-medal game, but it was such a cool experience. I got to play hockey with Jordin Tootoo...and bring home a silver medal."

I quickly walked back over to Michael. "You played in the AWG? *You played with Jordin Tootoo?*" My eyes lit up. I wasn't even born when Michael played in the AWG, but I'd grown up watching Jordin play big-league hockey. Suddenly, Michael seemed even cooler to me than before.

"You see, Davidee, not everything is about being the best. Heck, it's not even about winning. It's about trying...and if you don't try, you'll never really know if you can win or if you're the best." Michael reached out his hand, offering me the crumpled piece of paper. I slowly took the flyer from him.

"Thanks, Michael," I said. I continued down the hallway to my next class. Somehow, my steps felt lighter than usual.

After school, I walked home alone because Jason was playing hockey at the monument with our other friends. I had a lot on my mind and couldn't focus enough to play that night. When I arrived home, my anaana was standing in the doorway.

"How was your day, honey?" she asked. "I thought you'd be out playing hockey with the boys."

I shrugged and said, "I dunno. I've been down lately. There's no point in playing when it's always against the same people here in town. It's a bummer to not have other teams."

"Sounds like you're looking for a challenge," Anaana said.

I frowned and replied, "Yeah. Michael thinks I should try out for Team Nunavut. He says I could compete in the AWG, just like he did a hundred years ago." I knew it wasn't a hundred years ago, but I always poked fun at Michael's age because of the old Bravo he drove to school. "Michael thinks I have what it takes." I showed my anaana the crumpled Artic Winter Games flyer.

Anaana smoothed out the flyer and read it slowly. "If this is something you're serious about, you'd better get practising," she said. "Let's go!"

"Let's go? Where?" I asked, confused.

"I'm going to get groceries. I can drop you off at the monument so you can practise with Jason and the boys," she suggested. I grabbed my baseball cap and hockey stick and followed my anaana out the door.

CHAPTER 3
Alvin

For the next few weeks, I played hockey regularly after school with Jason and a few others. I was even doing push-ups and sit-ups in my room every night before bed. I wanted to be as strong as possible. I was so busy with hockey and exercise, I didn't have time for video games. That was okay. I needed to get better if I wanted to make the team.

Finally, the day came to go to the hockey tryouts. I was packed and ready to go, but I still had a bit of time before my flight. So when Jason asked if me if I wanted one more practice session, I happily agreed to meet him down at the monument.

"He shoots...he scores!" Jason yelled. He was having way too much fun scoring on me. "Keep your glove up. That'll make it easier to catch my lightning bolt slapshot!"

My glove was actually my baseball cap.

Snap! Another quick shot came from Jason. This time I grabbed the puck out of the air. "Nice!" Jason said. It was clear the last few weeks of hockey practice were paying off.

In the distance, a small plane was landing at the snowy Naujaat airport. In November, the runway was hard packed with snow, so the plane squeaked and slid up to the airport terminal. "Well, it looks like it's time for me to go to the big city, Rankin Inlet," I said with a laugh. Rankin Inlet was bigger than Naujaat but by no means a big city. I could hear my anaana calling my name in the distance. Jason and I walked over to the airport. We were greeted by my anaana, a few other family members, and Michael.

"Make me proud," Anaana wept. "I know you'll be great, whether you win or not." She squeezed me in a tight bear hug. She was sobbing, even though I was only going to be gone for a few days. How embarrassing. "And don't spend all of your allowance in one place!"

"Go get 'em," Michael said with a smile.

He gave me a fist bump. "Have fun in the big league!"

"Good luck, Davidee!" Jason waved as I climbed the steps to the small plane. I was the only passenger. This was common for flights leaving Naujaat. The plane usually made one or two more stops on the way to Rankin Inlet. I wished Jason was coming with me. When I'd asked him, he just laughed and said, "No way, man. You've got what it takes. I just play hockey for fun."

The plane rumbled down the runway, picked up speed, and began to lift off. Within a few moments, Naujaat was a small dot on the white, barren tundra. Before I knew it, the plane was making its descent to Baker Lake. It only stayed for a few minutes as a small group of people got on the nearly empty plane.

"Hey, Davidee! I missed you, buddy," came a familiar voice.

"Alvin!" I exclaimed as my friend plopped down in the seat beside me. We did our secret handshake.

It had been a year since I had last seen Alvin. We'd been close friends in Naujaat. Then Alvin's family moved to Baker Lake. I'd been looking forward to seeing him all week. We were even going to stay at Alvin's *anaanatsiaq*'s house together during the tryouts.

"I thought you would've gotten taller," Alvin laughed. Alvin and I were the same height and even kind of looked the same. People in Naujaat used to confuse us for brothers all the time.

"Funny, I thought you would've too," I joked, elbowing him. I was glad to be back with my friend. "So what do you think of these hockey tryouts? I hear there are some amazing players from Baffin Island." Baffin Island was always a powerhouse of hockey talent. Usually, half of Team Nunavut came from Iqaluit. They had two arenas.

"Well, there are always good players at the AWG tryouts. We just have to be better!" Alvin said. He was always very positive. If I was honest with myself, I'd stopped trying at hockey after Alvin moved away.

"Those guys from Baffin Island don't know how to skate hard, and don't even get me started on the Kitikmeot kids!" Alvin continued. I hoped that was true. I knew all kids said stuff like that about players from other regions. Making the team as a goalie was always very challenging. It meant stopping a lot of pucks during tryouts.

The plane began making its descent to Rankin Inlet, a hamlet over three times the

size of Naujaat. Rankin Inlet was home to a brand-new arena and even had a paved runway at the airport. Suddenly, feelings of doubt rushed through me. *Why am I here? Why did I leave my house? I could be at home right now playing video games instead of embarrassing myself!*

As the wheels on the airplane screeched against the tarmac, we slowly came to a stop. We'd landed in Rankin Inlet for the AWG hockey tryouts.

"I can't believe we're here, Davidee," Alvin said excitedly. "We're really trying out for Team Nunavut!" We grabbed our hockey equipment from under the plane and headed over to the arena. As we walked, Alvin said, "We're in the big league now."

CHAPTER 4
Tryouts

We were on the ice shortly after arriving in Rankin Inlet. There was no time to waste.

The head coach of the AWG hockey team was named Tony. He was a local hockey legend who'd played in the Ontario Hockey League. He had also played on the AWG team with Michael and Jordin Tootoo.

Tony said, "All right, everyone, welcome to the AWG tryouts. I'm going to let you know now that we only have room on the team for twelve skaters and two goalies." I swallowed. From the chatter on the airplane, I knew there were at least five kids trying out for goalie. Tony continued, "That means you need to play and skate hard this weekend if you want to wear the Nunavut jersey."

Tony was a solidly built, tough-looking coach. Even though he'd been retired from hockey for a few years, he could still move quickly around the ice and had one heck of a slapshot.

Tony had the players form a line at centre ice. That made it easy for him to size us up. I was one of the smaller goalies at the tryout.

Then we were split into two teams to play a scrimmage against each other. We would play three full periods. Players would rotate on and off the ice so Tony and the other coaches could see everyone.

I was assigned to play the third period of the game. *As long as I don't let any goals in, I'll be fine*, I told myself.

"I'll take it easy on you!" Alvin laughed as he skated out to centre ice. He played centre, and he was going to take the opening faceoff. The puck dropped, and the game was on. Normally, I loved watching my friends play hockey. But I was far too nervous to enjoy it that day. I watched helplessly from the bench while other goalies played the first and second periods. By the end of the second, my team was leading 3-1.

With the third period about to start, I skated down to my team's net. I banged my stick against both goalposts, backed into the net, and looked down the ice. "Who on Earth is that?" I said out loud. I couldn't believe my eyes. The goalie I was playing against towered over the net at the other end of the rink. From across the ice, he locked eyes with me, lifted both of his arms, and let out a loud roar. *Is this guy for real? Is he trying to intimidate me?* I wondered. It was working.

A few minutes into the period, Alvin rushed down the ice toward me on a breakaway. *Crack!* With a quick snap of his wrist, he scored a goal on me in the top left corner of the net.

"Hey, I thought you were going to take it easy!" I yelled to Alvin, who was already celebrating with his scrimmage team. The score was now 3-2.

"You've got to be on those," Tony yelled to me from the bench. "Make yourself big, like a polar bear on its hind legs!" I nodded back in agreement.

I got this, I told myself. For the next 10 minutes, my team made shot after shot at the other end of the ice. But the other goalie seemed invincible. No matter how hard my teammates tried, he was like a brick wall. He stopped every single shot. I couldn't help but be impressed.

Then, out of nowhere, there was another breakaway back toward me. This time, it was Alvin's teammate, a kid named Josie. He came across the blue line, did a quick

deke, and slid the puck toward the back of the net. I felt it *thunk* in my glove. Saved!

My team cheered, and even Alvin gave me a thumbs up. But I couldn't rest too easy. We were only ahead by one goal with just under a minute left.

I just have to survive the next minute without letting in another goal, I promised myself. Then Jimmy, a speedy kid from Kugluktuk, started to bring the puck up toward centre ice. Instead of skating toward me, he flipped the puck high in the air toward the net and skated off for a line change.

The puck was unpredictable, bouncing like an Arctic hare across the ice. I began to make myself bigger, standing up straight and puffing out my chest. As I reached for the bouncing puck, I almost missed it. For one heart-stopping second, I imagined Jimmy's half-hearted attempt landing in the back of the net. In that long slow-motion moment, I imagined I was back at the monument in Naujaat blocking Jason's shots with my Canadiens cap. I smacked the puck away from the goal.

Coach Tony blew his whistle, and the game was over. I cheered along with the other players, but I felt my throat tighten as the big goalie from the other team skated right up to me.

"Luke, right?" I asked the massive kid. He was a 15-year-old from Iqaluit, the oldest boy trying out for the team. "Good game."

"Nice save," Luke said sarcastically. He stood beside me as the players gathered at centre ice. "You almost let a Kitikmeot kid score from centre ice. You must be from Kivalliq." He was clearly trying to get under my skin.

Tony stood in front of the players. "I saw a lot of hustle out there. Some of you were playing really well physically. Some were playing well mentally." The coach continued, "Some of you took advice well too. Now let's take 10, and then we've got a skills session this afternoon."

It was over so fast! I couldn't believe how quickly the weekend of tryouts flew by. I hoped I'd done enough to prove myself. I was pretty sure Luke and I were the strongest goalies. Luke was bigger, but I was faster.

The day after tryouts, Alvin and I slept in. The coaches were going to post the teams on the arena door at noon.

Alvin's anaanatsiaq's house was right across from the arena. He and I were sluggish getting up and could feel aches and pains from the tryouts.

"Well, I guess we should go see." Alvin yawned and poked me with his foot. I was half asleep on the floor and pulled the blankets over my face, even though it was nearly noon.

"Do we have to? Can't we just go right to the airport?" I grumbled.

"You can, but I want to see the list," Alvin said. "Do you know how sweet it would be if we made the team? The Arctic Winter Games are in Fort McMurray, Alberta, this year. I heard they have every kind of fast food there. Fried chicken, pizza, and... CHEESEBURGERS!"

I pulled the blankets off my face. "They have cheeseburgers in Fort McMurray?" I was up now. "Let's go see if we made the team."

We walked out of the house. Even from across the road, we could see a white piece of paper stapled to the arena's door, blowing in the wind. *That must be the teams list.* I took one look at Alvin, and then we bolted for the arena.

"You didn't even move that fast in practice," I grunted as I caught my breath.

"Very funny, Davidee," said Alvin. "What does it say? Did we make the team? Are we going to the Arctic Winter Games?"

I found our age category on the paper and started reading:

AWG Bantam Boys Hockey Team
- **Jimmy (C)**
- **Josie**
- **Alvin (A)**
- **Edmond**
- **Charlie**
- **Pascal**
- **Luke (G)**
- **Daniel**
- **Noah (A)**
- **Joel**
- **Sam**
- **Louie**
- **Jonah**
- **Davidee (G)***

Alvin jumped up and down and let out a loud "Yeehaw!" followed by some hooting and hollering. He'd made the team, and he was excited. Not only that, but he had an "A" beside his name. That meant he was an alternate captain of the team, a huge honour. While Alvin celebrated, I calmly looked over the team list. My heart leapt when I saw my name, but then….

"What does that star beside my name mean?" I asked.

"It means you're the backup goalie," a deep voice said from behind me. I slowly turned around and saw Luke towering over me. "You're not the starting goalie,

because I am. Did you really think you'd have a chance at being the number-one goalie?"

I didn't know what to say.

"Don't be such a jerk, Luke. We're all on the same team now," Alvin said happily.

"We might be on the same team, but I'm the starting goalie. That's all that matters," said Luke. "Have fun riding the bench, Kivalliq." He cackled as he walked away.

Alvin and I walked back to his anaanatsiaq's house. I was excited to be on the team but rattled by my confrontation with Luke.

The next day, Alvin and I flew home. We had just a couple of months to train on our own before the Arctic Winter Games in Fort McMurray.

CHAPTER 5
Practice

When I arrived back in Naujaat, the first thing I wanted to do was play video games alone. I couldn't exactly explain why.

To my surprise, when I walked into my bedroom, there was a Nunavut flag hanging above my bed.

I turned to see my anaana standing behind me in my bedroom doorway. "Do you like the redecorating I did?" she asked. "Do you want to go to the arena to practise?"

"I love it, but I just want to hang out today and stay inside," I told her.

Anaana looked at me, confused. "Is everything all right?" she asked.

I shrugged. "I'm fine. Just...I just need some time alone, okay?"

Anaana raised her eyebrows. "Okay," she replied. "Take some time to relax. Then I want to hear all about tryouts."

I smiled. I appreciated my anaana. She could get my butt going when it was necessary, but she also understood that I sometimes needed to be alone with my thoughts.

"I'm setting a timer," she warned. "You can have half an hour to play video games."

Well, she *sort* of understood.

A little while later, I heard the oven timer go off and saved my game with a sigh. Time to tell Anaana what happened. Getting to be on the team wasn't as impressive as she and everyone else in Naujaat seemed to think.

I sat down at the table, where Anaana had laid out some apple slices.

"Hey there, Team Nunavut!" she said.

"Please don't call me that," I frowned.

"Why not?" she asked.

"Because, Anaana, I'm the backup goalie. I won't even be playing at the AWG." I groaned. "Luke is so much better than me. And bigger than me! He fills the whole net without even trying. I don't need to practise ever again. It's not like I'll ever even see the ice. Everyone will laugh at me for being the kid on Team Nunavut who never even played!"

Anaana gently touched my shoulder. "Come on, *irniq*," she said. "How do you think your coach made it to the OHL? Do you think professional hockey players make excuses like that? No. They get out there, practise, and get better. So many kids would love to play for Team Nunavut and represent their communities at the AWG."

I groaned again. "I just wish Luke wasn't such a jerk! I don't think I'd mind riding the bench as much."

Anaana handed me a cup of tea. She said, "If Luke is a better goalie than you, you just need to work harder. And if he's a jerk, just be overly nice to him."

"What do you mean by 'overly nice'?" I asked.

"Be nice to Luke even when he's being mean to you," Anaana suggested. "And be nice to your teammates, so they can see the difference between a bully and a good guy. Plus, who knows, maybe Luke is going through something and taking out his frustration on you."

How did Anaana always know what to say? I got up and hugged her. She was right. This was no time to feel sad. The Arctic Winter Games were just a few months away.

"You know, Anaana, I think I'd better go practise," I decided.

When I arrived at the monument, Jason was making a big windup for a powerful slapshot. *Slap!* The puck soared through the arch. "You know, it's harder to score if there's a goalie in the net," I called out. I held up my baseball cap and walked toward the arch.

"Hey, I heard the news. Congratulations," Jason said. "You made the team. That's amazing!"

"Well, I didn't quite make the team," I told him. "I'm the backup goalie."

"So what?" Jason replied. "You made the team. Who knows? Maybe if the coach sees something in you, you'll get to be the starting goalie."

"I don't think so, buddy," I said. "The starting goalie, Luke, is from Iqaluit. Is he ever good…and tall." I felt sad even thinking about being a backup goalie to Luke. "I'll never be the starting goalie."

"Never say 'never,' Davidee," Jason said firmly. "You never know! You might get the starting job if Luke gets hurt or something."

"You just said 'never say never,' but then you said 'never,'" I chuckled. I stood in the net with my baseball cap at the ready. "Give me your best shot."

Slap! A hard slapshot whizzed through the air and right into my hat.

From that day on, I remained focused on becoming a better goalie and preparing for the Arctic Winter Games that were just a couple months away.

CHAPTER 6
Heading to Alberta

A couple months later, I walked up the steps to the plane. I couldn't believe it was already time to go to the Arctic Winter Games! I turned and waved to the small group of friends and family who had come to wish me luck.

"Don't come back without some hardware!" Jason called out.

"Time to see if you can win!" Michael cheered.

"Just do your best! I'll miss you!" Anaana called out with tears in her eyes.

I was in for a long flight to Fort McMurray, with a few stops along the way.

The first stop was in Baker Lake to pick up Alvin. Alvin walked onto the plane decked out in his Team Nunavut gear. All of us players had had Team Nunavut gear shipped to our communities.

"Hey, Kopak, good to see you, buddy," Alvin greeted me. "You're looking really fresh in your gear." I was wearing the same Nunavut-branded clothing: a red-and-white jacket, a yellow scarf, and a blue toque.

"Good to see you too, Alvin. Your practice videos have been amazing! You know the teams at AWG always bring it." I knew Alvin had been practising because I'd seen his TikTok videos over the last few months.

After a few more stops around the Kivalliq region, the plane finally travelled west to Alberta. The inside of the plane sounded like a summer storm. The chatter was like rain, and the bouts of laughter were like thunder. The players from Baffin Island were on a different flight. They'd be landing at the same time. We were all excited, not just to play hockey, but also for the adventure of heading west to Alberta. But I couldn't help but let a hint of dread creep into my thoughts. I couldn't get the words "backup goalie" out of my mind or stop thinking about how Luke was such a jerk. *Stay positive*, I reminded myself as the plane began its final descent.

We crowded the windows to catch a glimpse of Fort McMurray. The white-covered forest and raging Athabasca River made for quite

the view. But so did the towering office buildings, roads that looked like they'd been laid out on a grid, and different types of fast-food restaurants.

"Cheeseburgers, *niam!*" Alvin said, pretending to wipe away drool. The airplane's wheels screeched to a halt on the runway, and we slowly pulled up to the terminal. A massive coach bus pulled up beside the plane to pick us up.

"Whoa, this so cool!" Alvin exclaimed. He couldn't believe that a fancy bus was going to pick us up right from the airport.

"Get used to it," I told him. "When we get to the NHL, this'll be normal for us." We quickly walked to the bus and climbed the steps. That was the first time most of us had been on such a big, luxurious bus. It was filled with comfy seats and mounted TVs. We were getting more excited by the minute.

A few moments later, the plane from Baffin Island landed, and the rest of the team came up to the bus. Alvin and I were sitting at the back. I secretly hoped that Luke somehow missed his flight, but no such luck. He walked onto the bus and looked down the aisle at Alvin and me. He was so tall, I thought his head might hit the ceiling.

"Who said you guys get the back of the bus?" he challenged.

"Take a seat, Luke," Tony snapped.

Luke rolled his eyes at me. "Oh well, all the good players sit at the front anyways." He thumped down into one of the seats near the front of the bus.

"Everyone listen up," Tony called out. The rest of the players quickly quieted down and found their seats. "Now, I know all of this is new for a lot of you: coming to Alberta, this fancy bus, staying at a school, meeting all the other Team Nunavut athletes. I know you're all excited."

He was right. I could barely hold still because of the excitement, even with Luke being a jerk. I thought about how the teams all got put up in school gyms and classrooms, like camping but indoors. It would be pretty cool to camp out with Alvin and our new friends. I just hoped Luke was in a different room.

"And I know you all want to explore the town and eat fast food. The reality is we're here to play hockey and represent Nunavut." The bus turned off the highway and started down busy roads lined with restaurants and stores. "So that means no fast food. No staying up late. We brought healthy food to eat while we compete. And you're all to be on your best behaviours."

Soon the bus slowed down and pulled into the school parking lot. The school's welcome sign read:

WELCOME, TEAM NUNAVUT!

Well, that was pretty cool. Backup or not, I was part of the team. And Team Nunavut had just arrived at the Arctic Winter Games.

CHAPTER 7
Cheeseburgers

"All right, boys," Tony said. "Classroom 301 is our home away from home. Go on in and pick yourselves a bed. No swapping once you've chosen."

I groaned. We were all in the same room? It was cool that I could hang out with Alvin and Jimmy and the guys, but Luke would be right there too. Ugh. Both Luke and I had our hockey equipment slung over our shoulders. He pushed ahead of me to get into the classroom first. Inside, I saw that instead of desks, there were rows of cots with sleeping bags on top.

Luke threw his equipment on the floor and

bellyflopped onto one of the beds right in the middle of the room. He didn't even check with anyone else first. It was like he owned the place.

"Who says you get first pick of the beds?" I snapped. I didn't really care which bed Luke had, but I was sick of him being a jerk.

"Because I'm a real member of the team, and you're a benchwarmer. You know, maybe if you focused more on how to be a better goalie and less on who gets which bed, you would be the starter," Luke said. The other guys were wandering in too, and they were keeping their distance from us. Luke rolled over onto his back and continued, "Don't you get it, Davidee? I'm the starting goalie. I'm under a lot of pressure to make big saves during important games. I can't be worried about people on my team trying to steal my job. So your job is to be quiet and let me handle it."

"*Your* team? *Your* job?!" I demanded. "Get over yourself, man. Coach says you're the starter, fine. I saw you play, and you were really good. I respect that. I just want to help out the team any way I can." I tried to keep my voice from shaking.

For a moment, Luke just stared at me, looking surprised. I threw my stuff down on a bed at the far side of the room and stormed out. The other guys let me go without a word.

The practice before our first game did not go well.

I had some ice time, but whether I was on the bench or the ice, I felt like our whole team was out of synch with one another. It's like we were playing different games. Coach Tony looked frustrated as he called out drill after drill.

"Way to let that goal in from centre ice," sneered Luke after the puck danced off my glove and landed in the net behind me. I couldn't believe I missed that stray slapshot.

"Come on, guys! We have to play as a team!" Coach shouted. My face burned with embarrassment.

After practice, I dumped my gear on my bed and headed out of the school. I didn't want to face Luke again. As I walked outside, I could hear familiar voices calling my name. Alvin and Jimmy stood on the school's front steps. "Davidee, where are you going?" asked Alvin.

"I just need some fresh air," I told them.
I looked around and saw some of the other players standing around outside the school.

Some of them were by themselves, and some were in groups of two or three. Everyone looked nervous. I frowned. It was weird. All the guys were wearing Team Nunavut jackets and toques, but we didn't look like a team. Maybe it was because of the bad practice.

I thought about what my anaana had said: "Be overly nice." I had an idea. I turned back to Alvin and Jimmy and said, "Actually, I'm going to get some cheeseburgers. Do you guys want one?" I knew what Coach Tony had told us, but I also knew that Alvin and I had been dreaming of cheeseburgers. The other guys might not be up for breaking the rules, but maybe he would be. I'd be warming the bench anyway. What harm could it do?

"Yeah!" Alvin said. "Jimmy and I are going down to the gym. They said it's open for us to use. But we could definitely eat some cheeseburgers after!"

"*Atii!*" Jimmy agreed.

"We'll cover for you if the coach asks where you are," Alvin added.

"Got it," I said. I headed down the busy streets of Fort McMurray in search of some good cheeseburgers.

I'd been walking for quite a while when I saw a fast-food restaurant with a giant cheeseburger-shaped sign that read:

THE BEST BURGERS IN ALBERTA!

I walked in and pulled out the allowance money I'd been saving for months.

"Yes, um, I'd like to order...uh..." Part of me wanted to order a few burgers and go find somewhere quiet to enjoy them. I liked having time alone with my thoughts. But I'd promised to bring burgers back, and we'd have to find a spot to eat them without the coach seeing us. I didn't want Luke around either. He'd probably give me a hard time. *What if I'm not the only one there? Luke can't give everyone a hard time.*

"Come on, kid," the cashier pressed.

"Twenty-four cheeseburgers," I finally said.

"Is this a joke?" The cashier looked around like she expected to see the rest of my team hiding behind me.

"And fries," I added. "Twenty-four orders of fries too."

It took a little while, but the cashier passed me two large, heavy bags. Both bags were dripping with grease but smelled heavenly. I raced back to the high school with a bag in each arm. I couldn't wait to dig in.

When I got back, I could see some of the guys still hanging around outside. Alvin and Jimmy weren't there, and neither was Luke. Then I saw the coach sitting outside with some of the chaperones. That means he wouldn't be in our room.

"Hey," I said to the guys outside. "I've got cheeseburgers for everyone. Party in Room 301?"

The guys cheered, and we hurried inside. The rest of the team formed a circle around me without even discussing it, like they were hiding me and the bags of burgers in case any of the coaches saw. As soon as we got to the room, I sent a text message to Alvin:

I HAVE UNLIMITED CHEESEBURGERS AND FRIES. IN ROOM 301. TELL THE TEAM. DON'T TELL COACH!

Not five minutes later, my teammates started entering the room. They couldn't wait for a cheeseburger.

"Coach will lose it if he knows we're having a cheeseburger feast," Jonah said as he plowed a burger into his face.

"This is so epic, Davidee!" Alvin exclaimed. He couldn't contain his happiness. Most of the team was spread out around the room eating burgers and fries. Suddenly, Luke walked in.

"I could smell the burgers from down the hall." He smiled as he looked around the room. "Who bought these burgers and went against what the coach said?"

"I did," I said with my mouth full of juicy, greasy cheeseburger.

"I should've known it was a goalie's idea," Luke chuckled. He picked up a burger and took a bite. "Thanks, Davidee. This is awesome!"

Was Luke just nice to me? He didn't even call me "backup goalie." Maybe this is what Anaana meant when she said to be overly nice? This was going great. I felt so happy.

After the feast, everyone sat around the packed room chatting and laughing. Then Jimmy said, "Coach wants us out front for a meeting at five o'clock. That's in 10 minutes."

Everyone started to get ready. Many of them thanked me and gave me high fives.

"That was really cool, Davidee," Luke said. "I can't believe you bought enough burgers for the entire team." He paused, thinking. Then he said, "And also, you know...when you're in goal and someone is coming down on a breakaway, you need to hold your glove up higher. And keep your elbow out. Otherwise, your form's pretty good."

I stared at Luke, but he was already headed out the door. "Let's go," he said. "We don't want to be late for our meeting."

CHAPTER 8
Round Robin

Five teams competed in the bantam boys ice hockey division: Nunavut, Yukon, Northwest Territories, Alberta North, and Alaska. The teams were split into two divisions for a round-robin tournament. The top teams from each division would play for gold. The second-place teams would play for bronze.

Team Nunavut played hard and beat Alberta North 1-0 in their first game.

As the backup goalie, I got to play a little during warm-ups and spent the rest of the game opening and closing the bench doors for line changes. But that was okay. We were finally playing like a real team, and I was part of it.

On the bus ride back to the high school, Coach Tony called back to me. "Hey, Davidee. I need you up here at the front. We need to have a talk." I was nervous but walked up the aisle and sat down beside him.

"What is it, Coach?" I asked shyly.

"Can you explain this?" He held up a cellphone and flipped through some pictures on Facebook of the boys having their cheeseburger feast. Some of them had even tagged their posts with "#ThanksDavidee." My face went hot.

"What did I tell you guys about fast food? We need to be in tip-top shape if we want to do our best," Tony reminded me.

"I know, Coach. But before you get mad, I can explain—"

"I know why you did it, Davidee," Tony interrupted. "I know you were having a hard time fitting in with the team, especially getting along with Luke. Being the backup goalie can be tough. I get it."

My jaw dropped. *What? Coach isn't mad at me?*

Tony continued, "To be honest, you've done a lot to bring this team together. Usually, there's a divide because the players are different ages and come from different communities. Somehow, your cheeseburger feast made Team Nunavut become, well, a team." He sounded sincere and proud. "Keep doing what you're doing on and off the ice. Let's keep winning."

"Will do!" I replied.

Coach Tony looked at me for another moment. "And Davidee? Don't break any more rules. You get a pass this time. But next time, you're on a plane home. Got it?"

I grinned. "Got it."

Over the next five days, Team Nunavut practised and played hard. With a 5-0 win over Alaska, we secured our spot in the gold-medal game against Team Yukon. Our entire team was thrilled to be performing so well.

Luke and I were walking into our classroom after our most recent win. He turned to me and said, "They're showing a movie in the gym tonight. Some of the guys are going to go. Do you want to?"

"Yeah!" I said. I couldn't believe how well Luke and I had been getting along. It

was like the icing on the cake of going to the gold-medal game.

I thought about my shop teacher, Michael, who had had this same experience back in 2000. I remembered what he had told me: "If you don't try, you'll never really know if you can win or if you're the best."

CHAPTER 9
The Gold-Medal Game

With the gold-medal game about to begin, I could feel the growing intensity in the arena. The stands were completely filled with screaming fans waving Yukon and Nunavut flags. A lot of other AWG athletes from different sports and teams were scattered throughout the arena.

The players for Team Nunavut and Team Yukon were lined up across our respective blue lines, awaiting the singing of the national anthem. "Wow, this is the big league!" Alvin shouted in my ear. It was getting hard to hear as the crowd in the arena became louder.

"Are you nervous?" I shouted back. Alvin raised his eyebrows high.

I felt calm. It was weird. I knew Luke would be the star of the show, but I wasn't upset about it anymore. I was part of the team, no matter what. I knew I'd gotten better over the last week, and I wouldn't trade this experience for anything. Even if I did wish it was me playing today.

After the singing of "O Canada," the two teams skated over to their benches. Coach Tony gathered our team closely and offered some words of encouragement. "Well, team, we're here. This is the big league. For these three periods, I need you to play your hardest. If you can do that, we'll bring home the gold!" Our whole team cheered. The gold-medal game was about to start.

Luke skated down to his net and banged his stick against both goalposts. Then he glared down the ice at Team Yukon's goalie, Ronnie. It was the same intense look he gave me during tryouts. Ronnie was about the same size as Luke but moved quicker from side to side in the net.

I made my way down the bench to sit by the door I was used to opening and closing during games. Within the first minute of the game, a Yukon player rushed down the ice on a breakaway. *Slap!* Before I could even catch sight of the puck, the buzzer sounded, and the Yukon fans went wild. Luke had completely missed the puck on what should've been a routine save. Team Yukon was leading 1-0.

A few moments later, the unthinkable happened. Team Yukon was again zipping down the ice with its top two forwards. Nunavut's defencemen were nowhere to be found. It was a two-person breakaway. As both forwards came toward Luke, they separated a little. With a quick pass from left to right, Team Yukon scored another goal. The sound of the buzzer was deafening. Team Yukon was now leading 2-0 in the gold-medal game. Team Nunavut had no offence or defence. Luke was our territory's best goalie. He hadn't let in a single goal all tournament but he let in two in the first period.

For the rest of the period, Team Nunavut's game improved a bit. We didn't let in any more goals, but we still had quite the uphill battle if we wanted to win. The buzzer sounded. The period was over.

The team was sitting in the change room during the first intermission. No one was saying a word.

"Time to wake up, team!" Tony warned us. "We can't hang our goalie out to dry. We need to be strong on defence and even stronger on offence!" Our coach was desperate to get our team motivated. "I've been here before, boys. Let me tell you, we can still win this. I know it's scary, that big crowd and those big expectations. But you're the same guys from practice yesterday, right?"

"Right," our team mumbled.

"You're the same guys who mopped the floor with Alaska, right?" Tony asked.

"Right!" our team said a little louder.

"You're the same guys who had a secret cheeseburger feast right under my nose, right?" Tony asked with a smile.

For a moment, everyone was stunned. I was the only one who knew Tony knew about our secret. Then Luke roared, "RIGHT, COACH!" and everyone laughed and stomped their feet.

"Then let's get out there and BE THOSE GUYS! Let's bring home that gold medal!" Coach Tony shouted. Everyone cheered.

During the second period, it was like a different Team Nunavut showed up on the ice. We were faster, our passes were more accurate, and our shots were more challenging.

"I'm open! I'm open!" Alvin called to Pascal. He slapped his stick on the ice, waiting for a pass. As the puck flew

across the ice, it landed right on Alvin's stick. *Snap!* Alvin scored a goal within the first minute of the second period. The score was now 2-1. Now Team Nunavut was only down by one goal. The boys continued to lay on the pressure. Shot after shot, Team Nunavut controlled the game. Team Yukon started looking tired. The rest of the second period was back and forth up and down the ice. The clock on the scoreboard ticked down, and the second period was over.

Team Nunavut quietly sat in the change room during the second intermission. We had fought back, but we were still behind by one goal. Now we were starting to feel the pressure. The fans were getting louder and louder as the final period of the gold-medal game was drawing near.

"They look really tired out there. You guys got this!" I cheered from the corner of the change room. The rest of the team looked at me in shock. As the backup goalie, I hadn't said much, and they were all surprised to hear me speak. I started banging my stick against the brick wall of the change room. "You can do it. I know you can," I chanted.

"WE can do it!" Luke said. He also started banging his stick. "We're all in this together." Soon, the entire team was banging their sticks and making a bunch of noise. "Let's go get that gold medal...as a team!" Luke shouted. The team rushed out of the change room. Luke's comment made me feel like I really was part of the team.

The intensity remained high during the third period. "Keep putting the pressure on!" Coach Tony called out from the bench.

Team Yukon was launching shot after shot at Luke. Suddenly, he jumped on the puck as it bounced around in front of the net, desperate to stop the play. *Pop!* "Oww!" Luke screamed as he grabbed his ankle. He lay on the ice for a few moments. When he tried to get up, he couldn't put any pressure on his right ankle. "Owww! I'm hurt really badly!" he moaned. He leaned on Alvin and hobbled over to the bench. He'd be out for the rest of the game.

"Davidee, you're going in!" Coach Tony pointed down the bench at me. I was his backup goalie and now the only goalie. I nodded at my coach and skated to the net.

I can be the best. I can win, I chanted to myself. I thought about my family and friends back home. I thought about Michael. I wanted to make them proud. I knew that I had to stay focused and make some great saves.

When the third period resumed, Alvin and Jimmy skated down the ice toward Ronnie. He looked gigantic in his net. "Alvin, I'm open!" Jimmy called for a pass in front of the net. With a quick tap of the stick, the puck slid right through Ronnie's legs. The buzzer sounded. The score was 2-2, a tie game. Then I started to feel some real anxiety, even before facing a single shot.

Team Nunavut won the next faceoff and skated fiercely down the ice. Suddenly, Ronnie looked smaller in the net. Alvin took the puck and blazed through the entire Yukon team and, with a quick deke... *snap!* Alvin scored again to give Team Nunavut the lead, 3-2. Team Nunavut cheered loudly, and so did the fans.

The announcer said in a deep voice, "One minute left in the game!" Team Nunavut was just 60 seconds away from winning gold. I watched the seconds tick away on the scoreboard. *Just another 30 seconds*, I told myself.

In a final effort, Team Yukon pulled their goalie so they could put another player on the ice. They moved the puck quickly up the ice, pushing past Team Nunavut with ease because of their extra player.

Then, it happened. The puck ended up just a few feet from me and the net. One of the Yukon players raised his stick, winding up for a big slapshot. *Crack!* The shot was loud and travelled through the air toward me.

Elbow out, glove up. Just like Jason and Luke—my friends—had taught me. I reached. *Slap!* The puck slammed into my glove, and I closed my fist around it. I had made the final save of the tournament and helped my team when it mattered most.

The buzzer sounded, and the game was over. Team Nunavut jumped and cheered loudly as they piled up at centre ice. Luke slowly hobbled over to the pile of players and came right up to me. "Amazing job," he panted. "You played like you're on the Canadiens. We did it together!"

Team Nunavut had won the gold medal.

CHAPTER 10
Bringing Home the Gold

I looked down at the shiny gold medal hanging around my neck. I was wearing my brightly coloured Team Nunavut gear, including my game-worn jersey that hadn't yet been washed. I felt happy. I smiled looking out the airplane window as I landed in Naujaat.

What an incredible experience. I made the team, played in the gold-medal game, and made some friends along the way.

In the airport, my family and friends were waiting for me.

"I missed you so much, Anaana!" I exclaimed. I gave her a long hug and then showed her my gold medal. She beamed at me with pride.

"Nice gold medal," Jason said. He jokingly tried to snatch it from me. I gave Jason a high-five and then walked over to Michael.

"Wow, Davidee. I watched Alvin's TikTok video of the gold medal game. You really played like you were the best. You played like a winner." Michael smiled.

I was happy to be back in Naujaat with my family and friends. From that day forward, I focused on the important things in life: playing hockey, being nice to others, eating cheeseburgers, and playing video games...once in a while.

Inuktitut Glossary

The pronunciation guides in this book are intended to support non-Inuktitut speakers in their reading of Inuktitut words. These pronunciations are not exact representations of how the words are pronounced by Inuktitut speakers. For more resources on how to pronounce Inuktitut and Inuinnaqtun words, visit inhabiteducation.com/inuitnipingit.

anaana ah-NAH-nah	mother
anaanatsiaq ah-NAH-naht-see-ahk	grandmother
atii ah-TEE	come on
irniq EER-nik	son
Naujaat NAH-oo-yaht	community in Nunavut
niam NEE-ahm	yummy

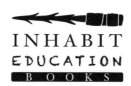